W9-BSU-023

OAK RIDGE PUBLIC LIBRARY
Civic Center
Oak Ridge, TN 37830

OAK RIDGE PUBLIC LIBRARY
Civic Center
Oak Ridge, TN 37830

In memory of Opa – *V.L.*

The Tsarevna Frog is a traditional Russian folk tale, retold here in a shortened version.
Many people know its counterpart *The Frog King; or, Iron Heinrich*,
collected by the Brothers Grimm in the early 19th century.

The Frog Bride copyright © Frances Lincoln Limited 2007
Text copyright © Antonia Barber 2007
The right of Antonia Barber to be identified as the author of this work has been asserted by her
in accordance with the Copyright, Designs and Patents Act, 1988 (United Kingdom).
Illustrations copyright © Virginia Lee 2007

First published in Great Britain in 2007 and in the USA in 2008 by
Frances Lincoln Children's Books, 4 Torriano Mews,
Torriano Avenue, London NW5 2RZ
www.franceslincoln.com

All rights reserved

No part of this publication may be reproduced, stored in a retrieval system,
or transmitted, in any form, or by any means, electrical, mechanical, photocopying,
recording or otherwise without the prior written permission of the publisher
or a licence permitting restricted copying. In the United Kingdom such licences
are issued by the Copyright Licensing Agency, 6-10 Kirby Street, London EC1N 8TS.

British Library Cataloguing in Publication Data
available on request

ISBN: 978-18457-476-0

Illustrated with oils

Set in Calisto MT

Printed in China
1 3 5 7 9 8 6 4 2

JP Barber
11/2008 010820736 $17.00
Oak Ridge Public Library
Oak Ridge, TN 37830

The Frog Bride

ANTONIA BARBER

Illustrated by VIRGINIA LEE

OAK RIDGE PUBLIC LIBRARY
Civic Center
Oak Ridge, TN 37830

F

FRANCES LINCOLN
CHILDREN'S BOOKS

There was once a King with three sons who decided that
they should all be married. "Fire an arrow into the air,"
he told them, "and seek your bride where the arrow falls."

The first son's arrow landed in the courtyard of a nobleman's
mansion. The prince was delighted and proposed at once to
the nobleman's proud daughter.

The second son's arrow landed in the garden of a rich merchant.
His daughter was foolish but very pretty, so the prince offered her
his hand in marriage.

But the youngest son, whose name was Ivan, was not happy.
He dreamed of marrying for love, not at his father's whim.
So he fired his arrow into the marsh lands, hoping that it
would never be found.

The King was angry. He sent Prince Ivan to find his arrow,
telling him not to return without it.

For many days the young prince searched and found it
at last in a clump of water lilies. Beside it sat a very small,
very ugly frog.

As Ivan bent to pull out his arrow, the frog stared at him
with its big frog eyes. It opened its wide frog mouth and croaked,
"Marry me!"

Ivan was horrified. "I can't marry a frog," he protested.

But the frog croaked, "I am your destiny."

So the Prince picked it up and, holding it at arm's length, carried it home.

When he told his father what had passed the King said, "Destiny is destiny!" and told him to marry the frog.

The Queen was unhappy. She did not want her youngest, handsomest son married to a frog. She decided to set the brides three tasks, to see if they would make wives fit for princes.

First she gave each bride a length of cloth, telling her to make a shirt fit for the King.

The nobleman's daughter told her maid to do it.

The merchant's daughter did it herself, very clumsily.

Ivan felt sure the frog would fail, and went off to bed.

But while he lay sleeping, a strange thing happened.

The little frog took off her frogskin and grew into a beautiful maiden. She cast the cloth from the palace window, where it was swept away by the wind. Before dawn, back came a splendid, embroidered shirt. The maiden put on her frogskin again and sat croaking beside it.

The King threw aside the first two shirts in disdain, but the frog bride's shirt he deemed fit for a state occasion!

Next the Queen told the brides to bake a fine loaf.

The first two brides suspected some magic and sent a servant to spy on the frog bride. But she saw the servant peeping and tipped her bread dough into the firebox of the stove. The spy told the other brides, who did the same so that their loaves were burnt.

When the spy was gone, the frog once more took off her frogskin. She mixed fresh dough and threw it from the window.

Before dawn it came back as a crisp, golden, beautifully decorated loaf.

The King said the first two loaves were uneatable, but the frog bride's loaf he declared fit for a banquet!

Now, Prince Ivan was also curious about the fine shirt and had stayed awake, watching unseen. He was astonished when he saw the frog take off her skin, and fell deeply in love with the beautiful maiden. *The next time she changes*, he thought, *I will burn that hideous frogskin and make her for ever my peerless princess.*

For her third task, the Queen asked the King to arrange a banquet. "Each bride must dance," she told him, "to prove that she is fit for life at court." *Here is one task*, she thought, *which a frog cannot do.*

Ivan was dismayed, but the frog bride croaked, "Trust me."

When the banquet began, she was nowhere to be seen. The brothers mocked him, saying that his bride did not dare to come. But even as they laughed, a fine coach drew up and from it, dressed like a princess, stepped the beautiful maiden.

Everyone marvelled. "She is surely some enchantress," whispered the first bride, and the second answered, "We must follow her every move!"

So they watched like hawks and saw the frog maiden pour the dregs
of her wine into her left sleeve. They did the same. Then they
saw her put tiny bones from the roast swan into her right sleeve.
Again they copied her.

After the feast, the King asked each bride to dance. As the
nobleman's daughter raised her arms, the swan bones flew out and
caught the King in the eye. As the merchant's daughter spun around,
dregs of red wine flew out and spattered across the Queen's robe. .

The King and Queen were not pleased!

Then the frog maiden began to dance.

As she turned, clear droplets of wine streamed from her
left sleeve and settled in a sparkling lake beneath her graceful feet.

When she turned the other way, the tiny bones flew out of her right sleeve.

Circling around, they grew into white swans, skimming the surface of the lake. The guests were enchanted and the maiden won the hearts of both King and Queen.

As she finished her dance, she looked about for Prince Ivan,
but saw no sign of him. With a cry of dismay, she ran from
the banquet hall, up the wide stairs to her room. She reached it
just in time to see the Prince throw her frogskin into the blazing fire.

Then she wept, crying, "Why, oh why could you not trust me?"

Ivan tried to take her in his arms but she tore herself from him,
leapt through the window and was carried away by the wind.

The young Prince was heart-broken: he fell into a deep melancholy.
The Queen sent for her wisest counsellor and told him the whole story.

"Why," said the old man, "this must be the Princess Vasilissa.
Her father is an Enchanter King who loved her dearly and taught her
his skills. But as she grew up, he feared that she was becoming
too powerful. In a fit of rage he transformed her, saying that the spell
could only be broken by a prince who would marry the frog."

"Tell me how to find her," pleaded Prince Ivan.

The old man sighed. "Your only chance," he said, "is to seek the help of her grandmother, the old witch Baba Yaga. She lives in a little hut on chicken's legs somewhere in the forests of the north."

Ivan set out the same day, and after many months of hardship came at last upon the strange little hut. He banged on the door, crying out, "Help me, Baba Yaga. I seek the Princess Vasilissa, whom I love with all my heart!"

The door opened a crack, and the old woman scowled at him.

The Prince poured out the whole sad story, but Baba Yaga only said, "You should have trusted her".

"I know it," said Ivan, "and if I find her, I will never doubt her again."

The old witch looked a little kinder.

"My granddaughter visits me each day," she said, "but she
will not enter if she sees you." She hid the Prince behind a curtain.
saying, "Take her in your arms and do not let her go!"

When Vasilisa arrived, Ivan did as he was told. But even as he put his arms around her, she changed once more into a small, slippery frog. He tried to catch her, but she was too quick for him.

At last he trapped her in a corner and knelt down to pick her up. But the little frog jumped over his shoulder and escaped him again.

Then Ivan realised that he would never catch her unless she chose to be caught. He sat on the floor and wept, saying, "If only I could have my beloved frog bride back again, I would love and trust her all my life!"

When he raised his head, he saw that the frog was sitting upon his knee, gazing at him steadily with her big frog eyes. Holding his breath, he reached out a hand, and she did not move.

Then he picked her up, very gently, and put her into his shirt pocket, next to his heart.

Now Baba Yaga smiled upon him. She lent him her magic carpet and soon the Prince and his frog bride were safely home.

The King and Queen were delighted to have their son back again. And when he told his mother that he was determined to marry his frog, she gave him her blessing.

The three weddings were celebrated with great splendour.
When the ceremony was over, Prince Ivan took the little frog
in his hands and kissed her wide frog mouth very tenderly.

At once the spell was broken and the wise and beautiful
Vasilissa appeared in her true form.

The Prince and his Princess lived happily together ever after.
But the Princess never let her loving husband forget that his bride
had once been a very small, very ugly frog.

OAK RIDGE PUBLIC LIBRARY
Civic Center
Oak Ridge, TN 37830

NOV 26 '08